Margit
HOME FREE

KATHY KACER

Margit
HOME FREE

KATHY KACER

PENGUIN
CANADA

PENGUIN CANADA

Published by the Penguin Group

Penguin Books, a division of Pearson Canada, 10 Alcorn Avenue, Toronto, Ontario, Canada M4V 3B2

Penguin Books Ltd, 80 Strand, London WC2R 0RL, England

Penguin Putnam Inc., 375 Hudson Street, New York, New York 10014, U.S.A.

Penguin Books Australia Ltd, 250 Camberwell Road, Camberwell, Victoria 3124, Australia

Penguin Books India (P) Ltd, 11, Community Centre, Panchsheel Park, New Delhi – 110 017, India

Penguin Books (NZ) Ltd, cnr Rosedale and Airborne Roads, Albany, Auckland 1310, New Zealand

Penguin Books (South Africa) (Pty) Ltd, 24 Sturdee Avenue, Rosebank 2196, South Africa

Penguin Books Ltd, Registered Offices: 80 Strand, London WC2R 0RL, England

FIRST PUBLISHED 2003

1 3 5 7 9 10 8 6 4 2

COPYRIGHT © KATHY KACER, 2003

ILLUSTRATIONS © JANET WILSON, 2003

DESIGN: MATTHEWS COMMUNICATIONS DESIGN INC.

MAP & CHAPTER OPENER ILLUSTRATIONS © SHARON MATTHEWS

MANUFACTURED IN CANADA.

NATIONAL LIBRARY OF CANADA CATALOGUING IN PUBLICATION

Kacer, Kathy, 1954–
Margit, book 1 : home free / Kathy Kacer.
(Our Canadian girl)
For ages 8–12.
ISBN 0-14-331200-6

1. Refugees, Jewish—Ontario—Toronto—History—20th century—
Juvenile fiction. 2. Holocaust, Jewish (1939-1945)—Juvenile fiction.
I. Title. II. Title: Home free. III. Title: Margit, book one. IV. Series.

PS8571.A33M37 2003   jC813'.54   C2003-903871-5
PZ7

Visit Penguin Books' website at **www.penguin.ca**

For my husband,
Ian Epstein,
and my children,
Gabi and Jake

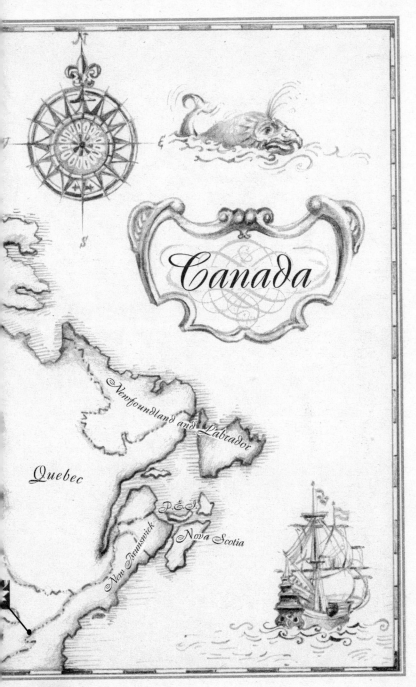

Canada

Newfoundland and Labrador

Quebec

P.E.I.

New Brunswick

Nova Scotia

 Marks the location of the story

MEET MARGIT

IT IS THE SPRING OF 1944 AND WORLD WAR II IS STILL raging. German leader Adolf Hitler and his Nazi army have pushed their way across Europe, aided by Italy, Hungary, and Romania. Canada, Great Britain, the United States, and other nations have banded together to try to defeat the Nazis. But the promise of peace is distant.

Eleven-year-old Margit Freed and her mother have managed to escape from their home in Czechoslovakia, which has been invaded by the Nazis, and have arrived as refugees in Toronto. But their arrival is bittersweet because they have fled without Margit's father. Like so many other Jewish people, he has been arrested and taken to one of the many concentration camps where Jews are being starved, beaten, and killed.

Few people in the world are willing to help the Jews or even to believe that they are being imprisoned and killed simply for being Jewish. Countries are reluctant to open their borders to escaping Jews. Even Canada, under Prime Minister Mackenzie King, has a strict policy that makes it very difficult for Jews to enter. The message to Jews trying to get into Canada is: "We sympathize with your situation, but at this time you cannot be admitted." Ultimately six million Jews perish during World War II. Between 1933 and 1945, Canada admits fewer than five thousand Jews.

In 1944, under pressure from many Jewish organizations, a handful of Jewish immigrants is allowed to come to Canada. But, to enter, they would have to meet special conditions, making it uncertain whether they would be permitted to stay. Many Jewish families hoping to find a warm welcome in Canada are saddened to find deeply rooted anti-Jewish feelings among some Canadians.

This is the situation in which Margit finds herself in April 1944. Although she is happy to have escaped from Europe with her mother, she is frightened because she does not know whether she will be accepted in Toronto. Will she make friends? Will people dislike her just because she is Jewish? And—most importantly— will she ever see her father again?

"*I don't see anything yet, Mamma,*" *cried*
Margit, as she stared out at the endless ocean,
straining to catch a glimpse of the approaching
harbour and the land that was to be her new
home. Grey fog blanketed the ship like a soft
comforter.

Her mother held the rail with one hand and
her belly with the other. For a moment she
closed her eyes, as the baby inside moved from
one side to the other, in time with the ship's
gentle roll.

"Keep watching, Margit," shouted Mamma, above the sudden blast of the ship's horn. "The captain says we're very close to Halifax now and we should see the port at any moment." She continued, "After we land it will take us two more days by train to reach Toronto."

Ha–li–fax. To–ron–to. In the past six months, these two odd-sounding names had become strangely familiar to eleven-year-old Margit Freed. And now, along with 280 other Jewish families, she and her mother were finally approaching the land that held the promise of freedom and safety for all of them.

"Our escape was a miracle," Mamma said suddenly. "We are so lucky."

Lucky! Margit frowned and glanced at her mother. Were they lucky because there was a war raging across the world, and they had been forced to escape from their home in Czechoslovakia? Were they lucky because everyone in the world seemed to hate Jewish people? Were they lucky that escaping meant having to flee without Papa?

Margit cringed inwardly at the thought of her father. Where was Papa? she wondered anxiously. Margit's mind travelled back to that terrible early morning when the soldiers had come to arrest her father, surprising the family with their loud, terrifying knock on the door.

"Out! Get out now!" the Nazi soldiers screamed, as Papa desperately fumbled for his glasses, trying to dress himself and grab a few personal belongings. There was no time for goodbyes.

Margit followed Papa outside to watch as he was loaded onto the truck and packed in with dozens of other men. He stood tall and proud, as if signalling to his family that he would be fine. Margit strained against Mamma's hand, knowing she dare not call out his name, for fear of drawing attention to herself. Right then and there, she and Mamma knew they had to leave or risk their own capture by the Nazis.

For several weeks after her father's arrest, Margit remained hidden indoors while Mamma snuck out to put the plans for their escape into place. Margit had little idea what Mamma was doing—where she went or with whom she spoke—but she was aware of secret groups that were helping Jews escape from the Nazi terror. The less Margit knew, the less she might be forced to tell if soldiers found her, her mother said. But each time Margit heard the shouts of someone being arrested on the street, she was certain it was her mother. Anxiously she watched the door, desperate to see Mamma's face and relieved when her mother returned at the end of each day.

Finally everything was ready. On the night of April 6, 1944, Margit and her mother waited at home for darkness before moving outside to the back of the house. Mamma felt along the wall for the one stone that was loose.

"Ah, here it is," she said, pulling out the stone and feeling behind for the black velvet purse. "It's all the money we have. Your papa and I have been putting it aside for an emergency. Who dreamed we would actually need it?"

Hesitating, Mamma dropped some money back into the purse before replacing it behind the stone. "I'll leave some here for Papa. He'll need it when he joins us," she said, fighting to keep back her tears.

It took them two weeks to cross through Austria and Switzerland into France, and from there into Spain. Fourteen harrowing days with little food, even less sleep, and the most intense fear Margit had ever known. How much money had her mother paid to the man who owned the truck, the farmer who drove the wagon, and the couple whose barn had provided shelter for them during their flight?

Once in Spain, her mother managed to make contact with local officials who were arranging safe passage for Jews to other parts of the world. Their task wasn't easy: these days few people cared about the Jews and their problems. Just when it seemed that no one would take them in, word had come that Canada was willing to accept a small number of Jewish people who had escaped the Nazi terror and who had not yet found a safe haven. But Jews allowed to enter Canada would have to meet certain conditions. They would be admitted only as refugees, not as immigrants. That meant there was no guarantee that they could stay. And they would have to pay $1,000 per family—a fortune! Of course, Mamma hid from Canadian officials the news that she was pregnant. There was no way they would have let her on the boat if they had known. Mamma had been sick the whole way over, but then so had so many others, with the ship's constant tossing and rolling.

As sunlight broke through the clouds, the fog began to disappear like smoke dissolving into the air. Margit strained to make sense of the vague shadows taking shape ahead.

"I see it!" cried Margit, pointing and jumping up and down excitedly. "Mamma, I can see the land."

"Yes, my darling. I see it, too. Come, we'd better go to our cabin and prepare for the landing.

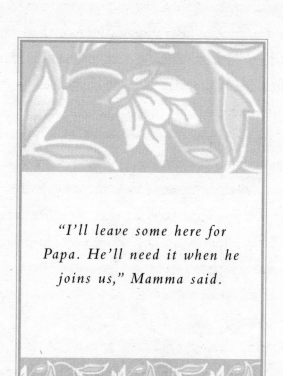

"I'll leave some here for Papa. He'll need it when he joins us," Mamma said.

We don't want to be left on the boat, do we?"
Mamma smiled as she moved away from the railing. She rarely smiled these days, thought Margit.
The war and leaving without Papa had worn her
down so much that trying to smile seemed
almost painful—as if she had forgotten what
happiness really was.

Margit rushed ahead of her mother, down the
steep stairs to the steerage class on the lower
deck and then around the twisting hallway to
their small cabin. Inside, she and her mother
quickly pulled together bundles of clothing and
the few personal possessions they had, while
trying to avoid bumping into each other in the
tiny room.

Margit caught sight of herself in the small
mirror above the cot. She reached up to smooth
her long, dark hair, brushing her curly bangs off
her forehead. Her green eyes flashed as she
glanced down at her wrinkled grey dress and
scuffed black shoes. How would she look next
to children in Toronto? she wondered. Would

she fit in? Would people like her? The questions whirled in her head as the ship's horn blasted again on the main deck. Docking was under way.

"Documents, please." The *official seated* behind the table barely looked up to acknowledge Margit and her mother.

Margit's mother placed the precious identification papers on the desk. The immigration officer wrote something in his logbook and then reached for the documents.

"Let's see, who we have here," the man said, finally raising his head. "Miriam Freed and Margit Freed. Is that everyone?"

Mamma quickly pulled her coat over her

stomach and nodded. Papa, thought Margit once more. We should be here with Papa.

With the help of a translator, the customs official began asking questions while Margit looked around. Everywhere, long lines of tired people waited for their turn to be questioned. Young children slept heavily on the shoulders of their parents. Others struggled under the weight of their bags. Grandparents limped stiffly behind their children. Everyone looked uncertain and out of place. Margit heard German being spoken and Hungarian and Czech, along with Italian, French, and other languages she didn't recognize. English words boomed out over the loudspeaker. Margit felt as if she had dropped in from another planet.

"You there." The immigration man was pointing at her. He smelled like cigarette smoke. Margit wrinkled her nose as she stepped forward, nudged by her mother.

"What's your name, young lady?" The man was smiling now. Margit caught the word *name*,

"But remember, your stay
may be temporary, and once
the war ends, you may be
asked to leave," said the
immigration man.

recognizing it from the English words she had practised on the boat. "My... name... Margit." She spoke slowly and carefully.

"Margit, eh? Well, that's an interesting name, young lady, but you might want to think of changing it to, say... Margaret—or *Maggie*. 'Maggie' sounds more Canadian."

Margit was horrified as she listened to the translator. Change her name? That was like changing who she was, changing her face, or her body! Maggie. She said the name out loud. She wasn't Maggie. She was Margit.

"There are lots of Canadian men fighting overseas in this war, you know," the immigration man continued. "I hope you realize how lucky you are to be here." There was that word *lucky* again, thought Margit. "But remember, your stay may be temporary. You are visitors. And once the war ends, you may be asked to leave. Don't make any trouble while you're here and everything will be fine." Mamma listened to the translator relay the warning, gulped and nodded.

The immigration man smiled again as he stamped their papers and handed them back to Margit's mother. "In the meantime, folks, welcome to Canada."

Mamma caught her breath as she collected the documents and pushed her daughter through the doors to the luggage collection area. She held the papers proudly for Margit to see. There, in capital letters, was the word *REFUGEE* stamped on each of their documents.

"Do you know what this means, Margit?" she asked, squeezing her in a tight hug. "It means we are finally safe. It means no one will harm us."

Margit was still troubled. If we're so free, she thought angrily, then why do I have to change my name?

CHAPTER N°3

"Toronto is next. All those for Toronto, gather your bags. The train will be arriving at Union Station in ten minutes. Toronto is next. " Margit was startled out of her sleep. She glanced at Mamma, whose eyes were still closed.

"Mamma," she said, gently rubbing her mother's shoulder. "Mamma, we're almost there."

Slowly Mamma opened her eyes and looked around, confused before the ever-present sadness set in. Her right hand moved to touch her wedding ring then settled on her stomach.

"Can you feel the baby, Mamma?" asked Margit. She wanted to be excited by this new life growing inside Mamma. But how could she be, when Mamma was so sad?

Mamma just shook her head ever so slightly then slowly stood and began to collect the bags. "How will we ever manage?" she muttered absently.

"Don't worry, Mamma. I'll help you." Lately Margit felt more like the mother than the child. Mamma seemed brittle, like a glass doll that might shatter if handled too roughly.

Stepping off the train, Margit was suddenly startled to be wrapped in the warmest bear hug she had ever known. Astonished, she pulled back and looked up into the round, soft face of Cousin Esther.

"Thank God you're here and safe at last." Cousin Esther was really Mamma's cousin, and a distant cousin at that. Esther was Mamma's grandmother's brother's granddaughter, or something like that. Margit always got it mixed up.

Still, Esther was family, and the only family they had in Canada. Cousin Esther and her husband, Joseph, were the ones who had written to Papa when war broke out in Europe, urging him to leave Czechoslovakia and come to the safety of Toronto. But Papa had resisted, and after his capture Mamma had contacted Esther for her help.

"Joseph, I found them," shouted Esther, as she continued to clutch Margit in the warm folds of her ample body. Instinctively, Margit reached up to return the hug. She felt as if she'd known Cousin Esther her whole life. "Come and get their bags, Joseph. Oh, Margit! Oh, Miriam! I can't believe you're finally here. I can't believe you're finally safe." Esther wiped the tears of joy from her own eyes. It was just the kind of greeting Margit and her mother needed.

As she left the train station, Esther continued chattering from behind the wheel of the car. Her Czech was quite poor, but its familiar sound was music to the ears of Margit and her mother. "We were so afraid that the Canadian government was going to change its mind and refuse to allow you to come," said Esther. "It happened a year ago with another group of Jews trying to get here, so it could have happened again."

"Mackenzie King!" Joseph spat the name out. Like his wife, Joseph was round and protective, grabbing Mamma's arm to help her walk and making sure she was safely positioned in the back of the car. "Some prime minister he is. He thinks that poor Jews from Europe will steal jobs from Canadians. And charging money for each of you to come here is robbery. The government is making a profit from your misery. Can't they see that they are saving lives by letting you and others in?"

"The tiny bits of information we receive from Europe are terrifying," continued Esther. "So many of our people are dying and suffering," she said, glancing at Mamma's face. Was Papa suffering too? wondered Margit.

"Stop, Esther," said Joseph. "They don't need to be reminded of what they've left behind." He turned to face Margit and her mother. "We found an apartment for you above a tailor shop. It's close to the synagogue and the market, and to the school where you'll eventually attend, Margit. It's small, mind you, but adequate."

Margit sighed deeply. It had been such a long time since Jewish children like herself had been allowed to attend school in Prague. She longed to be among children her own age, playing in a playground, running down the school corridor, and reading books.

"I've put some milk, bread, and other things in the kitchen. But tomorrow I'll take you to the market," continued Esther, as she pulled the car over to stop in front of a two-storey brick building. Joseph rushed to gather their bags and struggled to pull them up the narrow staircase to the top floor and into their new apartment.

Joseph had been right. It was small. The door opened to one tiny square living room, just big enough for the faded green couch and chair that Cousin Esther had managed to provide. On one

21

side the room opened to the kitchen, and on the other side was a bathroom. In the back, there was one bedroom that Margit and her mother would share.

"I hope you'll find it comfortable," said Esther, looking uncertainly at Mamma. "I know it's not what you've been used to, but...maybe if things change in the future, you'll look for something bigger and better." Margit knew that what she meant to say was that if Papa were to join them, they would need more space. But if it turned out to be just Margit, Mamma, and the new baby, then this would do. Mamma finally broke the deafening silence in the room with almost the first words she had spoken since arriving.

"The apartment is more than we could have hoped for. And you've done more to help us than we could have ever imagined. Thank you."

She has such hollow eyes, thought Margit as she watched her mother embrace Esther and

Joseph. They used to sparkle with pleasure at the smallest things, but now they're empty.

The bedroom had one larger bed for Mamma and one small cot for herself. Margit slumped onto the smaller bed, realizing only then how tired she was. She breathed deeply. Her first day in Canada and already she felt so confused. On the one hand, Canadians had joined the war to fight against Adolf Hitler and his terrible Nazi army. By doing that, Canadians were saving Jewish lives. On the other hand, Cousin Esther had said that the Canadian government didn't want Jewish immigrants to be here. And the immigration man had said they might be asked to leave when the war was over. Margit hoped that being in Canada meant she was safe and free. But if this is freedom, she wondered, why do I still feel so scared?

"We'll unpack tomorrow," said Mamma as she entered the room and lay down on her bed without even looking around the room. "We both need to sleep now, Margit darling."

Margit undressed quickly and climbed into bed. She fell asleep to the sound of Mamma whimpering softly in the bed next to her.

Margit awoke the next morning to the hum of sewing machines coming from the first floor. She stretched in her bed and looked around the room. The grey walls cast a gloomy shadow across the floor. One day I'll live in a room with yellow walls, just like the yellow sunflowers that grow by the side of the road outside Prague, thought Margit as she sat up in bed and looked around.

"Margit," called her mother from the kitchen. "Are you up? Get dressed quickly. Esther is already here to take us to the market."

The market! Margit rolled out of bed and pulled her stockings on and drew her jumper over her head. Maybe she could convince Mamma to buy some fabric for new clothes. Margit had watched some girls at the train station the day before. These Toronto girls wore colourful overalls with short-sleeved blouses. Her own clothes looked so foreign next to theirs. *How will I ever fit in if I can't even look like they do?* Margit thought, standing in front of the mirror and inspecting her appearance. Her shoes were black, sturdy, and laced to her ankles. Her stockings were heavy and woollen, and her dress reached well below her knees. Margit pulled her dress short and yanked her sleeves up above her elbows. That would be so much better, she thought, looking at herself again. Her green eyes flashed in the mirror as she tossed her long dark hair behind her ears, tying it back with a yellow ribbon. I'll talk to Mamma when we're in the market, she thought again.

"Margit, come for breakfast, now," her mother

called again as Margit headed out the bedroom door.

"Good morning, Mamma. I'm up and ready," said Margit, entering the kitchen. "Good morning, Cousin Esther."

"Oh, my dear Margit, you look so much better than you did last night." Esther was already chattering warmly as she reached over to kiss Margit on the forehead.

Mamma was sweating from the heat coming from the stove. She stirred the breakfast porridge, adding enough milk to make it smooth—just the way Margit liked it. Esther poured hot water into the teapot and added lemon and sugar. With the stove's warmth and the heat rising from the tailor shop below, their apartment was stifling. That's another reason to get rid of these woollen clothes, thought Margit as she quickly ate her breakfast and followed her mother and Esther out the door to the market.

Esther turned right outside the apartment and onto Spadina Avenue. Streetcars rumbled up and down the busy main street and cars beeped and swerved around pedestrians. It was Margit's first time on the streets of Toronto, and the sights and sounds of the busy city overwhelmed her. Margit rushed to keep up with Mamma and Esther. She didn't want to lose sight of either of them.

"That's the Anshei Minsk synagogue," said Esther, pointing out the impressive brick building close to the market. The six-pointed Star of David adorned the front entrance. Margit shuddered instinctively. The synagogue in Prague had been closed for several years. Esther chattered on about how most of the Jews of Toronto lived in and around this neighbourhood, on streets called Brunswick and Beverley. It reminded Margit of her Jewish neighbourhood back home, before all the trouble started.

The streets of Kensington Market were already crowded with vendors and dealers all looking to make a sale. Even though Canada was in the middle of the war, there was more food and more wares than Margit had seen in years. Painted signs hanging from the colourful stalls identified each of the owners. Margit painstakingly spelled out some of the names: Feldman Fruit, Nesker Butcher, Kaplan's Cheese. And periodically there were signs with names like Wong's Fish Market and Mario's Baskets and Barrels. So many cultures and countries were represented here. But Margit didn't need the names to recognize the stores. The smells alone were enough to let her know where she was. Sour cheese, baking bread, fish, and watermelon all combined into one satisfying aroma. And the sounds were overwhelming.

"Toe–may–toes! Bee–you–tee–ful toe–may–toes. Cu–cum–bers! Firm and sa–weet." The vendors sang their songs inviting customers into their stalls, holding apples and heads of lettuce underneath the noses of those who passed, competing with one another for a sale. War banners covered the sides of buildings with impressive paintings of Canadian soldiers marching in lines. Cousin Esther translated the headline: "'SUPPORT OUR BRAVE MEN OVERSEAS.'"

Esther approached the kosher-chicken lady and spoke to her in Yiddish, a language that Mamma knew, while Margit wandered farther into the marketplace, past the bakery with its smell of fresh bagels, past the barrels of salty pickles and stands of whole fish lying motionless on mountains of crushed ice. Up ahead a young boy walked past the dried fruit and nut stand while Margit eyed him curiously. He turned to look up and down the street as if watching for someone and then, when he thought no one was looking, he grabbed a handful of dried apricots with one hand and a fistful of peanuts with the other, and took off in Margit's direction. Margit just stood there with her mouth open. In a flash, the vendor was on the street striding towards her, his fists waving in the air. He stopped inches from Margit and, leaning his face down to hers, began to shout at her in English—words she didn't understand but whose meaning was clear. He thought she was the thief. Instantly Margit was transported back to another time and place. It was just like the Nazis coming for Papa. Margit shrank back from the vendor's screams and threatening glare.

"No, no, no," pleaded Margit, shaking her head forcefully while struggling with the few words of English she knew. "I...no...take." It was no use. How could she convince the man she was innocent when she didn't have the words to defend herself? Desperately she searched the gathering crowd, looking anxiously for Mamma or Esther, but they were nowhere to be seen.

"Let me help," said a voice beside her. Margit turned to see a young girl of about her age who had pushed through the crowd to stand beside her. *Help* was a word that Margit knew. The girl spoke quickly to the merchant, gesturing up the street and then at Margit. Margit could tell from the sign language and the few words she understood that the girl had seen the boy steal from the stall and then run off. As the girl spoke, the dark and angry scowl on the face of the vendor began to relax and disappear, to be replaced with uncertainty, confusion, and shame.

"Sorry, miss," he muttered, looking toward Margit. "There are too many thieves in the market."

Margit nodded. The tone in his voice and the embarrassed look on his face were easily understood. The man turned and walked back to his stall, motioning for Margit to wait.

Margit turned to the girl who had saved her and offered her hand. "Thank . . . you."

The girl flashed a warm smile. "You're welcome. I'm Alice. My parents own the flower shop over there, and I'm here helping them. Don't worry about the shopkeeper. He shouts a lot but he really wouldn't hurt anyone," she said, pointing behind her to a stall. The sign above it read "Donalds' Flowers."

The girl spoke too quickly for Margit to follow. But she understood the girl's name and responded with her own. Like Margit, Alice had long dark hair and friendly eyes. The two of them stood smiling at one another, not quite knowing what to do next, when the shopkeeper reappeared, carrying

"Let me help," said a voice beside her. Margit turned to see a young girl of about her age who had pushed through the crowd to stand beside her.

two small bulging paper bags.

"Here," he said, shoving the bags into the hands of the startled girls. Margit and Alice peered inside to find dried apples, raisins, and figs, along with cashew nuts and peanuts. "Sorry about the mistake," he muttered under his breath and turned and headed back to his shop.

Margit and Alice looked at one another then burst into laughter. "Would you like to come and see our store?" asked Alice, motioning to the flower stall behind her. Without waiting for a reply, she took Margit's arm and steered her over to the stand. The flower shop was beautiful, a rainbow of colours and scents.

"These are a rose, a tulip, and a carnation." As Alice identified each flower, Margit repeated the name in English.

"That's good," said Alice.

"What...is...this?" asked Margit, reaching out.

"A daffodil."

"Da–ffo–dil," repeated Margit. "And...this?"

"A lily. If you come again, I'll help you with your English. It won't take long to learn."

Help with English was just what Margit needed. "Yes... please help... English." Just then Margit heard the anxious sound of her mother's voice calling her. Margit turned to Alice and extended her hand once again. "I go. Thank you for... help."

"I'll see you soon," Alice replied.

Soon sounded like such a good word.

The next day and as often as she could in the weeks following, Margit returned to the market to meet Alice in the flower stall where she helped her parents after school. Margit looked forward to that time more than almost anything else in her day. For hours the two would wander through the stalls, touching and naming objects in English.

"That's a table and a chair," Alice would say clearly.

"And what is that and that and that?" Margit

was hungry to learn as much as she could. With Alice's help, Margit even practised buying things, a loaf of bread for Mamma or a special treat for herself. "One crushed ice with lemon syrup, please." Margit proudly counted out five cents for the refreshment.

Before long, Margit had graduated beyond single words to short sentences, and then to simple conversations. At times it was still difficult to communicate. Margit longed to ask Alice what young people thought about in Toronto and what was important to them. Classes would be stopping for the summer break in a few weeks. Mamma had decided that Margit would wait until September before beginning school. That way Margit could learn some English and be ready. Margit was desperate to know how others would accept her.

"Back home, in Czechoslovakia, my people were not wanted. Since the war, others . . . what is the word . . . hate us. And only because we are Jewish."

Alice nodded. Even though Alice herself was Christian, she seemed so accepting of the differences in their religions. "We've learned in school about Adolf Hitler and his Nazi Party. But we don't really know much about what is happening to Jews in Europe." She shook her head. "How can one group of people treat another group of people that way? And just because of a difference in religion? It makes me so sad."

"But that is why we are in Canada now," replied Margit. "In Canada life is good and we are all treated well."

Alice frowned. "I hope that's true for you, Margit," she said. "Remember, there can be cruel people everywhere in the world."

What did she mean by that? wondered Margit. She understood the word *cruel* but also knew it could mean different things. Sometimes she thought her parents were cruel to her if they didn't let her have her way. But the cruelty of the Nazis in Europe had gone far beyond simply being mean. The war was vicious and inhuman.

So many Jews were dying or being killed by Hitler's followers. Margit had been told that such cruelty didn't exist in Canada. But maybe Alice was talking about something else, a different kind of nastiness that she didn't yet understand.

Margit said goodbye to Alice and started for home, thinking more and more about their conversation. She was still deep in thought when she entered the apartment to find Mamma and Cousin Esther seated at the table.

"Hello, everyone," said Margit in English. Margit tried to get her mother to practise her English whenever she returned from a visit with Alice. She would move through the apartment, naming objects and having Mamma repeat after her. More often than not, Mamma was a cooperative student, diligently echoing the strange-sounding words. But today, the look on her face stopped Margit from continuing. Margit knew that worried look. She had seen it so often in Czechoslovakia.

"What's wrong?" she asked, searching her

mother's face for information.

Mamma hesitated a moment. "It's a letter, Margit. We've received a letter from home."

"Is it Papa?" cried Margit desperately. "Has something happened? Is he hurt?"

"The letter is not from Papa. It's from Mrs. Radek, our old neighbour. When we arrived here, I wrote her in the hope that she would know something of what has happened to your papa. She was always good to us, even when other neighbours turned away."

"What does she say, Mamma? Tell me what's in the letter." Margit couldn't stand the suspense.

Mamma turned the page of the letter and scanned its contents. She opened her mouth to begin to read, then caught her breath and stopped. It was Cousin Esther who took the letter from Mamma, turned to the second page, and began to read aloud.

I pray this letter reaches you as I know you are desperate for news of your husband, Leo. I have tried with all my might to find out where he could be. But gaining access to such information is almost impossible. The best I can tell you is that the truck he was placed on was taken to the train station. Everyone boarded the train for a concentration camp to the east of here. We know that these places are not what the Nazis have claimed them to be. Jews are not being resettled there in new homes. They are being starved and tortured and killed.

I know this is not the news you had hoped for. But I believe it is my duty to be honest with you, as I have always been. It's dangerous for me to write this to you, Miriam, but I don't care anymore. The world needs to know the truth of what is happening here. There are more and more rumours that the war may be ending and that the Nazis are on the run. And I pray this is true. In the meantime, be brave. Leo is a strong man and you must not give up hope. My love and best wishes to Margit. Tell her the apple tree in my yard has the most beautiful red apples, ready to be picked . . .

Esther stopped reading and the room fell silent. The only sound Margit could hear was the beating of her own heart, a sound so loud to her ears that she thought her chest might explode. The letter said that Papa had been taken to a concentration camp. But was it possible that he might be dead? She couldn't imagine such an outcome. Even as the horrible reality of the war in Europe was reaching Margit and her family, somehow she had to believe that such things were not happening to the people she knew and loved. Such things could not be happening to Papa.

Margit watched as her mamma's silent tears fell onto the table. Esther stroked Mamma's arms and looked deeply into Margit's eyes. "You heard what the letter said, Margit. You must be brave for your papa and for your mamma."

"No," Mamma said, raising her head. Margit startled at the sound of Mamma's voice. "You're not alone, Margit," she said, mustering more strength than Margit had heard for some time. "We must be brave for each other."

Margit flung herself into her mother's arms,

stuffing her fist into her mouth to stop herself from crying aloud.

"I just know Papa's alive, Mamma," she sobbed into her mother's shoulder. "I can feel it in my heart. The war will end soon and he'll come back."

Mamma stroked her head tenderly. "Keep believing that, Margit darling. Keep believing."

Margit turned and ran from the kitchen into the bedroom, where she threw herself down on the bed. Fiercely she pounded the mattress with one hand and stuffed the pillow against her mouth. Papa was alive. She knew it. She felt it. She would not accept anything else.

CHAPTER N°6

For weeks, Margit walked around in a daze, going through the motions of living but feeling shriveled up and alone inside. Even meeting Alice in the market seemed to lose its pleasure. It was Mamma who finally took charge. One morning, Margit awoke as usual to the music of the sewing machines below her. Her eyes ached from having spent most of the night crying again. Margit slowly pushed herself out of bed as Mamma entered the room.

"Margit, we need to talk." Margit nodded

vaguely. "Darling, you can't keep doing this to yourself. You can't give up like this. It's not what your papa would want from you."

At the mention of Papa, Margit felt the tears welling up again in her eyes. She couldn't speak and only nodded at Mamma. "I know how scared you are feeling, Margit," Mamma continued. "I feel it myself. But we have to go on with our lives. Do you understand that?"

Margit nodded again.

"So, this is what we must do. Each day, you and I are going to say a prayer for Papa. And each day, we are going to do something that he would be proud of. Is that a deal?"

Margit reached up to hug her mother tightly. It was good to have her strong mother back. Mamma was right. With or without Papa, Margit had to go on. What choice did she have? So she vowed to learn more English, meet new people, and prepare for the day when the war would be over and Papa would return to them.

Mamma went out that morning to get the

early edition of the morning newspaper, the *Evening Telegram*. Over a cup of lemon tea and a slice of buttered bread, she scanned the headlines, trying to make sense of the news in the world. By the time Margit entered the kitchen, Mamma was in a fluster, trying, with her poor English, to understand what was written. It was so difficult. Mamma spoke three languages fluently— Yiddish, Czech, and German—but her English was so poor. Margit tried to help, piecing together words that were familiar into an understandable sentence or two. But there was a difference between talking to Alice about everyday events and making sense of newspaper reports.

"'August 26, 1944. Allied forces drive north- ward and eastward toward Germany and Belgium. One hundred thousand Nazis flee from France. The Germans are withdrawing to a new defence line as the attack by the First Canadian Army gathers momentum and pounds the enemy from dusk to dawn.' I think all of that is good," said Margit hesitatingly. Alice had talked about rumours of a change in the war, a change that suggested the possibility of peace.

"Are you sure or do you just think?" said Mamma.

"I'm not sure, Mamma," Margit replied.

"Oh, this is so hopeless," cried Mamma impatiently. "Oh, I'm not angry with you, Margit," she added quickly, noting her daughter's distress. "I just need to know. I'll talk to Esther. Perhaps she can help me with these words."

Cousin Esther and Joseph were constant visitors to the apartment, bringing food, extra clothing, and even the occasional piece of furniture. Esther was always chatty and Joseph had a warm sense of humour. Margit looked forward to his visits. He always had a trick or two for her, like making a penny appear out of her nose, or finding a piece of chocolate behind her ear. It was almost like having a father around. And when Margit reached up to hug him, Joseph would lovingly squeeze her in return. Esther and Joseph had no children of their own, and they were growing to love Margit like a daughter.

"Joseph and Esther have been more generous than we could have ever hoped for," said Mamma one day after a visit. "But we can't live on their charity forever. I've been thinking about this for some time, Margit. And I've decided that it's time for me to begin working. We don't know how long it will be until your papa joins us." Margit took note of the catch in Mamma's voice as she mentioned Papa. "So," said Mamma, breathing deeply, "in the meantime I need to earn some money. The tailor in the shop downstairs has agreed to let me bring a sewing machine up to our apartment, along with pieces of material. I'll be making pockets for trousers and collars for shirts."

"Mamma, won't it be too much for you with the baby?" Margit was worried. Mamma's belly was getting bigger and bigger.

"I'll take care of myself, darling. Don't worry. And for every pocket and collar I make, the tailor will pay me fifty cents," said Mamma proudly.

"We'll be able to buy our own food, and maybe even some new clothes. I'm lucky that I can work here at home. But it does mean I will need more of your help, Margit dear. Soon you will be starting school, so I know that will also be difficult for you. But we have to pull together and help each other in whatever way we can."

School! The thought of starting school in Canada had seemed like a dream to Margit. Now the reality of walking into a new classroom was beginning to set in. Margit felt sick and excited at the same time.

Margit nodded at her mother and gulped down her own fear. "I'll do whatever you need."

CHAPTER N.º 7

"Class, please pay attention." Miss McCaul turned away from the blackboard to face the students in front of her. "We have a new student joining us, and I'd like to introduce her to you. This is Margaret Freed."

Standing next to Miss McCaul, Margit felt her face go red with embarrassment. "Miss..." she said haltingly. "My name is Margit."

The teacher glanced down at her attendance card. "Oh, sorry. Yes. This is *Mar–git* Freed. Margit is from a country called Czechoslovakia," she continued. "As you know, Czechoslovakia is in the midst of the world war. Some of your fathers, uncles, and older brothers may be fighting in Europe right now, defending the freedom of our country and all countries in the Alliance. Margit and her mother were lucky to escape and to be able to come here where they can be safe."

Stop! thought Margit. Stop talking about me as if I'm in a history book, or in a museum. In her mind, Margit remembered the times back home when she and her family had tried so desperately not to bring attention to themselves. Standing out in a crowd meant being singled out as a Jew, and that could mean being arrested like her father. Still, the faces on the boys and girls in front of her were curious, not hateful. Most of them looked friendly enough, even interested in her. Most importantly, Alice was there, smiling with encouragement and pointing to the empty desk beside hers.

"Yes, Alice," continued Miss McCaul. "I think having Margit sit beside you would be a

wonderful idea. Would you like that, Margit?"
Margit nodded, speechless, and moved to sit
down next to her friend.

The morning was a blur of strange textbooks
and instructions that made little sense to Margit.
Everyone spoke so quickly, and it was impossible
for Margit to grasp what was being said. Thank
goodness she had Alice next to her to help with
translation. I have so much to learn, thought
Margit weakly.

"All right, class," called Miss McCaul. "Take
out your language notebooks and complete the
assignment from the blackboard. Quiet, please.
There is no need for talking."

Margit raised her hand hesitantly.

"Yes, Margit?"

"Please Miss. I need pep—seal?" Margit struggled to find the word she needed.

"Pepper? Is that what you want? Salt and pepper? Whatever do you need with pepper?" Miss
McCaul looked confused.

"No, no," struggled Margit, shaking her head

furiously. "I need pep–seal." Oh, what was the word?

"I'm sorry, Margit. I still don't understand you." Margit heard snickering from several class-mates as her stomach churned. It was hopeless. Even Alice looked confused. In desperation, Margit looked around and grabbed the writing tool from Alice's desk.

"Pep–seal," she repeated. "Pep–seal. I need this."

"Oh, a *pencil*," replied Miss McCaul as several students giggled and pointed in Margit's direction. "Here you are, Margit," she said. "Don't worry, dear. The words will come easier with time. I have a suggestion. Instead of doing this assignment, why don't you try writing something in this journal." Miss McCaul placed the notebook on Margit's desk. "That way you can practise your English. Back to work, class."

Margit's face burned and she angrily wiped the hot tears from her eyes. Alice's sympathetic glance did little to comfort her. She felt so different and alone, like some strange animal on display in a zoo. There were other Jewish children in the class, but they had been born in Canada and didn't stand out the way Margit did. Margit grabbed the pencil, opened the notebook, and began to write furiously. Words poured out of her in anger and humiliation—in English and in Czech. Writing was cleansing. It wiped the bad feelings out of her body. When lunchtime came, Margit grabbed her bag and her journal, and ran outside to eat alone and write some more. It was exhausting trying to understand what everyone was saying. It was too hard to fit in. She *didn't* fit in. That much was clear.

"Hey, you." A voice interrupted her thoughts and Margit looked up to see two girls from her class standing in front of her. What now?

"You're Jewish, aren't you?" The taller girl nodded in Margit's direction as the shorter one kicked a stone with her shoe. Margit gulped and nodded.

"My mother says there are too many Jews here already and Canada shouldn't have let you in. It's your fault the world is in this mess anyway." Margit recognized the anger in this girl's eyes. She had seen it before, on the streets of Prague, in the eyes of girls and boys who had once been her friends. Margit opened her mouth but no words came. Once again she felt sick and alone.

"You can't even speak English, so what are you even doing here?" The smaller of the two girls kicked the stone menacingly in Margit's direction. Margit was cornered and scared. Were the girls going to hurt her? How could she defend herself against both of them?

"Leave her alone!" a familiar voice called from across the schoolyard. Margit looked up to see Alice striding across the field in her direction. She planted herself between Margit and the two bullies, hands on her hips and feet wide apart. "What do you think you're doing, Ellen? Margit's new here. Can't you be nice for a change?"

Margit's heart was still beating wildly in her chest. Ellen and the other girl hesitated a moment longer while Alice faced them squarely. Their eyes were narrow and hostile.

"Come on," said Ellen abruptly. "You're still a stupid Jew," she called over her shoulder as she stomped away, dragging her partner along with her.

Margit was shaken as Alice moved to sit next to her. For a moment the two girls sat in silence. Was this the cruelty that Alice had spoken about? Was Margit going to be hated everywhere in the world, just because of her religion?

"They're not all like that," said Alice, as if reading her mind. "I'm not like that."

Margit reached for Alice's hand and squeezed it gratefully. Once again Alice had proved to be her friend.

"Come on," said Alice, smiling. "I want you to meet some other friends."

Margit walked into her apartment and slumped onto the living room couch just as Mamma entered the room. The rest of the school day had been uneventful, but Margit still felt on edge.

"Margit, darling, I've been waiting to hear about your first day at school. Ah, your face looks so troubled, Margit. Tell me, what is it?" asked Mamma, as she sat down heavily on the couch, shifting her swollen belly to a more comfortable position.

Margit hated to burden her mother with her troubles. But before she could stop herself, she blurted out everything that had happened that day. She talked about what it was like to walk into the strange classroom, to struggle with the English language. She told Mamma about Ellen threatening her. She talked about Alice and how she had come to Margit's rescue. Finally, she talked about meeting some of Alice's friends, girls who seemed more friendly and welcoming.

"Part of me is so excited about going to school here," Margit said. "I mean, isn't that what we've been waiting for? To be in a country where Jewish people are free to go to school? But I'm so afraid, Mamma. I know it's not like it was in Prague. I mean, nobody is going to arrest me for being different. But I still hate what that feels like. There are some kids who are nice to me, and Alice is so kind. But already, there are kids who are making fun of me, and who are mean to me. How many more like that will there be? How will I ever fit in?"

Mamma paused a moment. "I'm not going to tell you that everything will be easy, darling," she began. "But I have such confidence in you and in your ability to make friends and learn new things. You already have a friend in Alice. And perhaps her friends will also become your friends. But you must believe in yourself as well. Above all, be proud of who you are and where you are from. That's the spirit that will help our people survive in Europe—pride in our Judaism, pride in our culture, and pride in our history."

It all sounded so simple when Mamma spoke. Of course Margit was proud of who she was. But the challenge was going to be in showing that pride to others, especially when she felt so different. Surely Mamma understood how important it was for a young girl to fit in.

"Did I ever tell you the story of what happened one day early in the war when I snuck out to find some food in town?" asked Mamma. "It was so dangerous then to leave our home, but without food we would starve and you were so frail. Your papa and I both knew it was worth the risk. I took some of the precious money we had and walked into town, pretending I was a peasant woman, shopping for food in the market. With a scarf on my head and my shabby clothes, I could easily pass for a Gypsy. I was just about to buy some milk, when who should walk up to me but Dasha Slaba. She and her husband ran a bakery where we shopped before the war. She was never a friend to the Jews in the village, and was one of the first to close her doors to us when the rules restricting the freedom of Jews were introduced. As soon as she looked into my eyes, I knew I was doomed."

"What did you do?"

"Well, I knew I had a choice. I could run, but police patrolling the market would have caught me in a flash—a woman like me. I could plead for mercy, but somehow I knew that was just what she wanted, and I couldn't allow her to see me beg. So I stood up as tall as I could, looked her straight in the eye, and said to her, 'Dasha, I am not less than you are. I breathe just as you do. I walk and I sleep and I think just as you do. You can turn me in, but remember my face and it will haunt you.'" Mamma paused and looked at her daughter, whose eyes were as wide as saucers. "And you know what she did? She turned and walked away from me. She never told the authorities. I bought the food I needed to keep us alive, and I returned home safely."

Margit let out a long sigh, not realizing that she had been holding her breath.

"So you see, my darling daughter, even if you look a little different from other children, or eat different foods, or pray in a distinct way, you are just as worthy as those around you. Never forget that." Mamma leaned forward to kiss Margit on the forehead. "And now I have a gift for you." Mamma walked into the bedroom and returned a moment later holding a bag in her hands.

Curiously, Margit reached inside and pulled out the bundle of clothes. Excitedly, she held up the navy blue overalls and matching flowered blouse. They were modern and brand new, just what she had wanted.

"Oh, Mamma, thank you so much. They're beautiful." Margit clutched the clothing to her chest and reached over to hug her mother. Mamma must have spent hours sewing the clothes when Margit wasn't around.

"Enjoy them, darling. And remember. Looking like everyone else is only part of belonging."

Margit was left alone to think about what her mother had said. She reached into her school bag and pulled out the journal that Miss McCaul had given her. Opening it to a clean page, Margit began to write down the things her mother had talked about. "I must be proud of who I am," she wrote. Margit looked at the words on the page, but still the uncertain feeling would not leave. Besides, she also knew that hundreds of thousands of Jews were standing up to the Nazis in the war only to be crushed. What would those Jews have said to her? Was it worth standing up for your differences? Margit wasn't sure.

CHAPTER N.º 9

A week later, Ellen tripped Margit on her way to the blackboard and shoved her harshly in the line for recess. Margit blinked back tears but didn't say a word.

"Come on," said Alice, who had witnessed the whole thing. "My friends and I are going to play skipping. We'll teach you a new game." Margit joined in the skipping game, easily learning the new verse. "Apples, peaches, pears, and plums, tell me when your birthday comes. January, February, March..." Alice's friends laughed at her strange pronunciation of the months of the year. But it wasn't a mean laugh. It was a friendly laugh that said, "You're a part of us and we like you."

Still, she couldn't seem to shake Ellen. After recess Margit found a note by the coat rack that read: *Go back where you came from, you stupid Jew.* Margit looked around but no one was there.

"What's the matter?" asked Alice, as Margit walked slowly to her desk.

"What? Oh, nothing," replied Margit. The fun of recess and being part of the skipping game disappeared. Margit was certain the note came from Ellen, although there was no way she could prove it. So what could she do? She couldn't keep running to Alice for help. Besides, Alice couldn't be there to protect her every minute. She wouldn't tell Miss McCaul. That would just feed into Ellen's belief that Margit was weak. She wasn't going to start a fight. That wasn't her style. So Margit bit her lip and did nothing.

Mamma was wrong. It wasn't about being proud of your past. It was about trying to wipe it out and pretend it didn't exist. If Margit could get rid of her European past, then maybe she could be like all the other children in her class. She desperately wanted to be just like them.

And slowly things were changing. As the months passed, Margit understood more and more of what Miss McCaul and others were saying. She followed the conversations of the children in her class and tried to imitate the way they spoke. She tried to dress the way they dressed and comb her hair the way they combed theirs. She answered questions in class and got caught up in math and science. She read books in English by Stephen Leacock and Robert Service. And at all costs, she tried to avoid Ellen.

One morning, a few months after Margit's first encounter with Ellen, Miss McCaul pulled Margit aside as she was entering the classroom.

"Margit, dear, I have a wonderful idea," she began.

"Yes, Miss McCaul," Margit replied. What now? she wondered.

"I've been reading through your journal, and I'm so impressed with how you have written about your life in Europe before and during the war." Since the first day of school, Margit had been writing something in her journal every day. It was the place to pour out her feelings, and a private place to practise her English. At the end of the day, Miss McCaul would collect the journals, correct them for grammar, and return them to each student. "I'm sure the rest of the class would learn so much from listening to you talk about your experiences. What do you think? Would you be willing to read your journal to your classmates?"

Margit froze, a phony smile on her face. *This can't be happening*, she thought. Just when she was trying to be like everyone else, her teacher was suggesting that Margit share with her classmates the very things that made her different from them—her past, the war, her Jewishness.

"Fine," continued Miss McCaul. "Take your seat and I'll let the class know."

"But, Miss..." Margit tried to talk but no words came out. Besides, Miss McCaul did not seem to be listening.

"Class, please pay attention," Miss McCaul announced, as Margit anxiously made her way to her seat. The students in the room raised their eyes from their work. "As you know, the journal entries that I ask you to do are private. I am the only one who reads them. Well, today we have something special. Margit's writing is an incredible account of the hardships she experienced in Czechoslovakia before escaping. It's something we should all hear. I'd like to ask Margit to please come to the front of the room and read some of her entries for the class. Margit?"

Miss McCaul paused and held Margit's journal out to her, inviting her to stand and face the class. Margit's stomach churned and she felt her face burn with shame. Now they were really going to hate her, she thought. Ellen would have all the ammunition she needed to make Margit's life miserable forever. But what choice did she have?

She couldn't run away or disappear. Saying no or making a scene would be just as humiliating.

"Margit?" Miss McCaul was waiting for her to respond. What Margit really wanted was for the floor to open up and swallow her whole. But instead, she found herself standing and walking slowly to the front of the room.

Alice squeezed Margit's arm encouragingly as she passed. I hope Alice will still be my friend after this, thought Margit as she took her journal from Miss McCaul's hands and turned to face the class.

"Why don't you begin here," said Miss McCaul, "and just read some passages over the next several pages."

Margit looked down at her journal. The letters swam in front of her eyes as she took a deep breath, cleared her throat, and began to read. "I was six years old when the war started, and eight years old when the Nazis marched into Czechoslovakia. But for years before that, I knew what it was like to be different, and to be hated because of that." Margit turned several pages and continued. "I remember the first day we had to wear the Star of David on our clothing. The six-pointed star had always seemed so beautiful to me. But the yellow cloth star with the letter "J" in the middle that we had to sew on every piece of clothing we owned was not beautiful. It branded us just like cattle.

"November 25, 1942. My friend Lilly disappeared today. People are saying that Lilly, her parents, and her two brothers were arrested in the middle of the night and taken away. Her father tried to organize a rally last year to protest the treatment of Jews in our community. That's why the Nazis wanted to arrest him—because he spoke out against the government. But why was Lilly arrested? She was ten years old. She did nothing wrong. I'm so afraid I'll never see her again.

"September 10, 1943. I remember watching as the Nazis shot an old Jewish man in the legs. First they made him wash the road in front of their

Margit looked down at her journal. The letters swam in front of her eyes as she took a deep breath, cleared her throat, and began to read.

cars. They shoved him onto the ground with a bucket and brush, making him scrub the cobblestones so they would be clean enough for their automobiles to pass. I counted eight strong soldiers with guns and one helpless old Jewish man with a bucket. After they shot him, the soldiers stood around, making sure no one would help him. I turned my head and walked home. I turned my back and walked away. What could I do?"

On and on Margit read, poring through the pages of her journal. She read about how she hadn't been allowed to play in the park, visit the zoo, go to the ice cream parlour or the cinema. She read about waking up to find that friends and family had disappeared overnight—imprisoned or perhaps having successfully escaped the country. She read about Papa's arrest and her escape with Mamma. Not once did Margit glance up. She was lost in her own writing and in reliving the war. Finally, she turned to the last page and read. "*Scared! Sad! Hungry! Bored!* That was my world. I am eleven years old and I am innocent. But this war sentenced me to a life without school, without food, without friends, without my father, without happiness. This is an ugly war—an ugly, horrible, disgusting war. When will it end?"

Margit closed the book and looked up at her classmates. There was complete silence as the children faced her. What do they think of me now? wondered Margit. Am I an even bigger freak in their eyes? Suddenly the entire class erupted into spontaneous applause. They cheered, they whistled, and they stood on their feet.

At the break, several children rushed up to Margit, nearly knocking her over.

"That was amazing, Margit. I had no idea what was going on for you," said one girl.

"Your escape was really something. I'm glad you got out," said another boy. "My dad's fighting in Europe with the Canadian army. I hope he helps a lot of Jewish people."

Alice grabbed Margit, squeezing her hard. "I'm so proud to be your friend," she whispered in Margit's ear.

Miss McCaul approached Margit, wiping tears away from her eyes. "Thank you for sharing your amazing life with us, dear."

Margit's head was spinning. She blinked in amazement. She had faced her classmates and shared her most difficult experiences. She had spoken strongly, honestly, and proudly. She had done well!

On the way out the door, Margit passed Ellen, who stood blocking her passage. Ellen was glaring and still looked as hateful as ever. Margit faced her squarely and looked deeply into her eyes. This time she wasn't about to flinch. Ellen hesitated a moment. "I still think that you're a stupid Jew," she said, as she whirled around and stomped out of the classroom.

Startled, Margit paused and closed her eyes. Then she took a deep breath and shrugged her shoulders. Well, she thought, I guess there are some people who will never change. Margit turned around, grabbed Alice by the arm, and pulled her out onto the playground.

CHAPTER N.º 10

"Mamma, I'm home." Margit burst through the apartment door. "Wait until you hear what happened at school today." Margit was bubbling over with the news of how she had stood up and talked about herself. But Mamma wasn't there; instead Joseph greeted Margit at the door.

"Your mamma is in the hospital," said Joseph.

"What!" cried Margit. "What happened? Where is she? Is she okay?" Margit's day was instantly forgotten as panic set in. But the expression on Joseph's face stopped Margit in her tracks.

"Don't look so worried, dear," said Joseph, smiling. "This is good news. Your mamma called Esther today right after you left for school to say she knew she was going into labour. Esther came over immediately and took her to the hospital. She had the baby early this afternoon, Margit. You have a brother."

The baby! Margit's mouth fell open as the news sunk in. There was a brand-new baby in her family—a boy. Margit had a baby brother.

"Well, don't just stand there," said Joseph, laughing at Margit's stunned expression. "Get your coat back on and let's go. It's time for you to meet the new arrival."

Margit flew out the door, practically dragging Joseph after her. She couldn't wait to see her mother and she couldn't wait to see the baby. At the entrance to Mount Sinai Hospital, Joseph paused to speak to a nurse. Children of Margit's age were not usually allowed up to the maternity floors. Margit overheard Joseph whispering about Margit's father and their situation. The nurse glanced at Margit, frowning at first. Then she closed her eyes and nodded, while Joseph pumped her hand furiously and grabbed Margit. Together they approached Mamma's hospital room.

"Come in, darling," called Mamma softly, as Margit knocked on the door. Slowly Margit pushed the door open, giving Esther a hug as she approached Mamma's bed. Mamma's eyes were tired but peaceful. In her arms was a tiny bundle wrapped in layers of blankets. Mamma moved one arm to pull Margit close and embraced her in a soft and gentle hug. Mamma smelled like medicine and sweat, but it was a sweet aroma to Margit. Finally, Mamma moved her arm away and opened up the blankets for Margit to see.

Timidly Margit looked down at the new baby. Her eyes moved over his dark, feathery hair, his tiny red face, and his hands balled up into small fists. The baby's eyes were shut and his mouth was making soft sucking noises.

"This is your new brother," said Mamma. "What do you think of him?"

"He's so wrinkled looking," blurted out Margit.

Mamma smiled. "He'll smooth out. Just give him some time. What shall we name him?"

Margit thought a moment. "Let's give him a simple name, something English, something Canadian. Let's call him Jack."

Mamma smiled again. "Yes," she said finally. "My late father, your grandfather, was named Yacov. It means Jack in English. It is a simple name but a good one. I think Jack is a perfect name."

The baby opened its tiny mouth and howled loudly.

"I think he likes it," said Margit, laughing along with her mother.

CHAPTER N° 11

Life at home was hectic with the new baby, but Margit quickly settled into her role as big sister. She loved bathing her brother, feeding him his bottle, and even changing his diapers. Best of all, she loved to make him laugh. It was just like a game. Margit would nuzzle her head into Jack's soft, round stomach, or pretend to bite his big toe. Jack would stare curiously at Margit, waiting to see what was next. And then he would grunt, open his mouth wide, and make the funniest laughing noises Margit had ever heard.

"Let me do it," Alice exclaimed one day when she was over visiting. Margit and Alice fought over the fun of making Jack laugh. And he never failed them. Margit often wondered who was enjoying the game more, Jack or she and Alice.

"Did you hear the news about the war?" asked Alice one afternoon as they played with Jack. "My dad said the Nazis are leaving their tanks behind and running away. He says they're being hammered. Do you know what that means?" Margit shook her head as Jack laughed again.

"It means they're losing badly. It means the war could be over soon. Oh, Margit. All the Canadian soldiers will be coming home. It's so exciting, isn't it?" She turned to Jack as he pulled on her long hair. "No more war, Jack!" She sang:

Whistle while you work
Hitler is a jerk
Goering's barmy, so's his army
Rub 'em in the dirt!

"Oh, you cutie, you have no idea what I'm saying, do you?" Jack just laughed and Alice joined in. Margit knew that Hermann Goering was the head of the Nazi air force. She wasn't sure what words like *jerk* and *barmy* meant, but one thing she was certain of: the city was full of anticipation about the end of the war and the defeat of the Nazis.

It was now the spring of 1945. One year had passed since Margit and her mother had arrived from Europe. Back then it had felt as if the war might go on forever. But these days the signs in store windows read: "The hour of success is near." Along with the smells of spring, the scent of victory was in the air. Even Mamma smiled more often, now that she had Jack. Life would have been almost perfect if only Papa were there.

One morning a few weeks later, Margit awoke to a new sound. Instead of the hum from the sewing machines downstairs, she heard loud noises rising from the streets. Margit moved to the window, trying to make sense of the gathering crowds as Mamma ran into the bedroom.

"Margit, it's over. The war is over! Germany has been defeated. Hitler has been defeated."

Margit rubbed her tired eyes, struggling to comprehend the news.

"Get dressed, darling. We're taking Jack outside." Mamma rushed from the room as Margit dressed quickly and joined her. Toronto was already going wild in celebration. Margit, Mamma, and baby Jack in his stroller joined the crowds of people, marching on the street and shouting, "The war is over! The war is over! Our boys will soon be home." Stores along Spadina Avenue had already pasted in their windows the front pages of the city's newspapers, whose headlines announced: "May 7, 1945—PEACE IS WON! NAZIS GIVE UP! SURRENDER DOCUMENT SIGNED."

Other stores were replacing their window displays with red, white, and blue streamers to match the colours of the Canadian flag. Loudspeakers mounted on the tops of cars and trucks blasted the Canadian national anthem.

Someone shoved a Canadian flag in Margit's hand and she held it high above her head, proudly waving to the passing marchers. Margit felt a new freedom, one she had never felt before. It was one thing to escape Europe and be in a free country, but now it felt as if the whole world was free at last. The whole world, thought Margit. Could the end of the war mean that Papa was free as well?

There was no school that day or the next. For two whole days the city rejoiced with fireworks and parades and celebrations. Margit and her family attended a special service at the synagogue where the rabbi gave a prayer of thanks for the end of the war and a prayer of comfort for all those who had been killed or died in the camps. Margit stuffed her hands into her ears so she wouldn't hear that part. Now more than ever, Margit needed to hold on to hope about Papa.

Without thinking, Margit settled back into her daily routine. She left for school early in the morning, after giving Jack his breakfast so

Mamma could sleep a little longer. After school, it was Margit's job to take Jack for a walk, then help Mamma with supper and do her homework. Margit ended her day by writing in her journal, closing with a daily prayer for Papa's safety.

Then came the day that started like any other. Margit was sitting in the kitchen trying to feed cereal to Jack, who was making a fuss, as usual. He hated being confined in the high chair. He waved his fists, squirming and wiggling so much that more cereal ended up on his head than in his mouth. Mamma had gotten up early and was finishing some work in the living room when the doorbell rang.

"I wonder who that is," said Mamma. "It's much too early for the tailor to pick up his sewing. I'm not even finished yet," she muttered, rising and moving to the door.

A postman stood at the door, holding out a dirty and crumpled envelope. "Are you Miriam Freed?" he asked. Mamma nodded. "Sign here, please."

Mamma signed the clipboard and closed the door, turning the letter over and over in her hands. Finally she tore it open and pulled out a single sheet of paper. Seconds later she gasped, cried out, and dropped to the floor. Margit rushed out of the kitchen holding Jack in her arms, to find her mother in a sobbing heap.

"Mamma," she screamed, putting Jack down and hurrying over to her mother. "Mamma, what's wrong? What is it?" Margit's heart pounded with fear, a fear she hadn't felt for so long.

Mamma could say nothing. Meekly she held the letter out for her daughter. Margit reluctantly took the page and looked down at it. One sentence jumped out at her as she grabbed her mother and hugged her with all her might. *I'm alive and I'm coming home to you. Love, Papa.*

AUTHOR'S NOTE

On April 6, 1944, a boat called the S.S. *Serpa Pinto* arrived at a port in Philadelphia, Pennsylvania, carrying 280 European refugees. In the months following, two more boats arrived carrying smaller numbers of refugees. Most of these passengers were Jews who had smuggled themselves through war-torn countries into Spain and Portugal, where they boarded ships for the safety of North America. On their arrival, they were quickly processed through immigration and bused to waiting trains that took them north to Montreal and Toronto, where they were admitted by the Canadian government as refugees. For the purpose of this story I have brought the arriving Jewish families directly to Halifax, Nova Scotia.

Although the government of Canada reluctantly allowed Jewish refugees to enter the country, it also had plans that would make it possible to find and deport them to Europe at any time during and after the war. Fortunately, these plans were never put into place.

Once the war had ended, families like Margit's were allowed to remain in Canada. Although for many the adjustment to Canadian life was difficult, these Jewish families found work and security, things they had not known since unrest began in Europe before the war. Over the next years they were joined by many more survivors of the Holocaust. These Jewish immigrants put down strong roots in Canada, turning hardship into opportunity and loss into dreams.

ACKNOWLEDGEMENTS

MANY THANKS TO CYNTHIA GOOD, BARBARA BERSON, AND THE CREATIVE TEAM AT PENGUIN CANADA. I AM THRILLED TO BE PART OF THIS WONDERFUL SERIES. THANKS ALSO TO CATHERINE DORTON AND ANNE HOLLOWAY FOR THEIR SUPPORTIVE INPUT AND INSIGHTFUL EDITING.

THANKS, AS ALWAYS, TO MY FAMILY: MY HUSBAND, IAN EPSTEIN, AND MY CHILDREN, GABI AND JAKE. THEY CONTINUE TO INSPIRE ME WITH THEIR LOVE AND THEIR FAITH IN MY WRITING.

Dear Reader,

Did you enjoy reading this Our Canadian Girl adventure? Write us and tell us what you think! We'd love to hear about your favourite parts, which characters you like best, and even whom else you'd like to see stories about. Maybe you'd like to read an adventure with one of Our Canadian Girls that happened in your home-town—fifty, a hundred years ago or more!

Send your letters to:
Our Canadian Girl
c/o Penguin Canada
10 Alcorn Avenue, Suite 300
Toronto, ON M4V 3B2

Be sure to check your bookstore for more books in the Our Canadian Girl series. There are some ready for you right now, and more are on their way.

We look forward to hearing from you!

Sincerely,
Barbara Berson
PENGUIN CANADA

P.S. Don't forget to visit us online at www.ourcanadiangirl.ca—there are some other girls you should meet!

1608
Samuel de Champlain establishes the first fortified trading post at Quebec.

1759
The British defeat the French in the Battle of the Plains of Abraham.

1812
The United States declares war against Canada.

1845
The expedition of Sir John Franklin to the Arctic ends when the ship is frozen in the pack ice; the fate of its crew remains a mystery.

1869
Louis Riel leads his Metis followers in the Red River Rebellion.

1871
British Columbia joins Canada

1755
The British expel the entire French population of Acadia (today's Maritime provinces), sending them into exile.

1776
The 13 Colonies revolt against Britain, and the Loyalists flee to Canada.

1837
Calling for responsible government, the Patriotes, following Louis-Joseph Papineau, rebel in Lower Canada; William Lyon Mackenzie leads the uprising in Upper Canada.

1867
New Brunswick, Nova Scotia, and the United Province of Canada come together in Confederation to form the Dominion of Canada.

1870
Manitoba joins Canada. The Northwest Territories become an official territory of Canada.

1784
Rachel

1862
Lisa

1885
At Craigellachie, British Columbia, the last spike is driven to complete the building of the Canadian Pacific Railway.

1898
The Yukon Territory becomes an official territory of Canada.

1914
Britain declares war on Germany, and Canada, because of its ties to Britain, is at war too.

1918
As a result of the Wartime Elections Act, the women of Canada are given the right to vote in federal elections.

1945
World War II ends conclusively with the dropping of atomic bombs on Hiroshima and Nagasaki.

1873
Prince Edward Island joins Canada.

1896
Gold is discovered on Bonanza Creek, a tributary of the Klondike River.

1905
Alberta and Saskatchewan join Canada.

1917
In the Halifax harbour, two ships collide, causing an explosion that leaves more than 1,600 dead and 9,000 injured.

1939
Canada declares war on Germany seven days after war is declared by Britain and France.

1949
Newfoundland, under the leadership of Joey Smallwood, joins Canada.

1896
Emily

1944
Margit

1885
Marie-Claire

1918
Penelope